THE SNOW ANGEL

A Red Fox Book

Published by Random House Children's Books
20 Vauxhall Bridge Road, London SW1V 2SA

A division of Random House UK Ltd
London Melbourne Sydney Auckland
Johannesburg and agencies throughout the
world

1 3 5 7 9 10 8 6 4 2

First published by
The Bodley Head Children's Books 1993

Red Fox edition 1995

Printed in Hong Kong

RANDOM HOUSE UK Limited Reg. No. 954009

ISBN 0 09 950261 5

THE SNOW ANGEL

Angela McAllister
Illustrated by Claire Fletcher

Red Fox

It was the first snow morning. Elsa made giant's footsteps to the frozen dewpond. She built snow castles, and she slid down the slippery slope.

Then she found a secret place. Elsa lay on the snow blanket and spread her arms like wings. She made the shape of an angel.

Elsa showed her friend Jack. 'This is where a snow angel lay,' she whispered. That Jack always thought her tales were true.

'I wish I could see a snow angel,' he sighed, 'more than anything in the whole wide world.'

The next morning Jack found Elsa. He was very excited.

'I saw her! I saw the snow angel last night, sweeping away the snowdrifts. And she gave me a wish and I rode the big rabbit. And it's true, I really did.' But Elsa just smiled. That Jack was always dreaming.

The next morning Jack looked everywhere for Elsa.

'The snow angel came again!' he said. 'She melted the ice with her breath. And she gave me a wish, and all the fish were flying fish, even that old whiskery. And I saw it, I really saw it.' But Elsa just smiled. That Jack was always telling stories.

The next morning Jack was waiting for Elsa.

'The swinging tree was so heavy with snow it was going to crash through the window, and the snow angel blew it all away. And she gave me a wish and all the icicles were made of sugar. And I ate one hundred and I really, really did.' But Elsa just smiled. That Jack was a good pretender.

That night a fresh snow fall covered the giant's footsteps and the castles and the slippery slope. Everything was buried deep. But, when Elsa returned to the secret place, an angel's shape still glistened in the snow. Were those the wings she had made?

Gently Elsa lay down.
She thought about
Jack. She shut her eyes
and made a wish. And
when she sat up the
snow wings began to
grow.

First little snow buds,
then long soft, white
feathers unfolded and
lifted her high amongst
the trees!

Up and up and Elsa
flew through the frosty
air. She shook the
branches, she stood on
the treetops, she
skimmed the stepping
stream. Then low
among the trees
someone was hiding.

And Elsa flew.

All morning she flew with the snow angel in and out of the blue shadows, until the sun began to melt her wings. One last swoop over the church spire then softly Elsa fell to earth.

Jack met Elsa at the slippery slope. He was very excited. 'I didn't see a snow angel this morning . . . I saw two!'

Elsa looked up through the snowflakes and laughed. Maybe that Jack knew a true thing after all. 'Come on then Jack,' she said, 'let's make giant's footsteps in this snow.'